Gimme a Break, Rattlesnake!

Schoolyard Chants and Other Nonsense

Gimme a Break, Rattlesnake!

Schoolyard Chants and Other Nonsense

gathered and written by
Sonja Dunn

illustrated by
Mark Thurman

Stoddart

Text copyright © 1994 by Sonja Dunn
Illustrations copyright © 1994 by Mark Thurman

First published in 1994 by
Stoddart Publishing Co. Limited
34 Lesmill Road
Toronto, Canada
M3B 2T6
(416) 445-3333

Canadian Cataloguing in Publication Data

Dunn, Sonja, 1931–
Gimme a break, rattlesnake!

ISBN 0-7737-5696-5

I. Nursery rhymes — Juvenile literature.
2. Rhyming games — Juvenile literature.
3. Children's poetry.   I. Thurman, Mark, 1948–
II. Title.

PS8557.U55G5 1994   j398.8   C94-930242-2
PZ8.3.D85Gi 1994

The origins of schoolyard chants are varied and difficult to
trace, therefore no credit denoting authorship has been
given to the rhymes in this collection.
The publishers will gladly receive information that will
enable them to rectify any inadvertant copyright errors or
omissions in subsequent editions.
When rhymes contain brand names or registered
trademarks, the publisher has denoted them by use of
uppercase letters.

Edited by Kathryn Cole

Printed in Canada

Acknowledgements

For generations schoolyard chants have been repeated and embellished in thousands of playgrounds by millions of children. They have made their way into books and lives and memories, and have provided children with empowerment and entertainment. They have spread to all corners of the world and have been adapted with amazing skill and creativity. The origins of some stem from long-forgotten history. Some owe their existence to a sense of fair play and others make no sense at all, except that they reflect a joy in the rhythms and manipulation of language. Still others mirror the often fractious nature of children as they learn to cohabit the schoolyard. The exuberance and fun found in each one is a testament to the spirit and resourcefulness of generations of children.

This collection is by no means complete and is largely the invention of many people. But here and there I couldn't resist the temptation to add new verses and a few rhymes of my own. I have enjoyed gathering, expanding, and remembering these chants with all my friends, young and old. Together we travelled back to those special skipping, clapping, ball-playing days and had the chance to be kids together. Thanks to my writing colleagues, to children from playgrounds across the country, especially those from Mary Immaculate Separate School in Chepstow, Tweedsmuir Public School in London, and Forest Hill Public School in Toronto. Very special thanks to Paul Dunn's class at MacLeod Public School in Sudbury, and to Paul for *Skateboard Sam* and *The Cookie Crumbles*.

Dan, Dan, the ragbag man,
Washed his face in a frying pan,
Combed his hair with a donkey's tail,
The cops came along
And put him in jail.

In jail they gave him coffee,
In jail they gave him tea,
In jail they gave him everything,
Except the jailhouse key.

Algie saw a bear,
The bear saw Algie.
The bear was bulgy,
The bulge was Algie.

Way down south
   where the bong trees grow,
A grasshopper stepped
   on an elephant's toe.
The elephant said
   with tears in his eyes,
"Pick on someone
   your own size!"

The lightning crashed
The thunder roared
Around the Union Station.
The little pig
Curled up his tail
And ran to save his bacon.

I went to the movie tomorrow,
I took a front seat at the back,
I fell from the floor to the ceiling,
And tripped on a hole in the crack.

Have you ever, ever, ever,
In your long-legged life
Seen a long-legged sailor
With a long-legged wife?
Have you ever, ever, ever,
In your knock-kneed life
Seen a knock-kneed sailor
With a knock-kneed wife?
Have you ever, ever, ever,
In your bow-legged life
Seen a bow-legged sailor
With a bow-legged wife?
Have you ever, ever, ever,
In your long-legged life
Seen a knock-kneed sailor
With a bow-legged wife?

I had a little chicken
And she wouldn't lay an egg,
So I poured hot water
Up and down her leg.
And she wiggled and she jiggled
And she stood on her head
And the funny little chicken
Laid a hard boiled egg.

Not last night, but the night before,

Twenty-four robbers came to my door. This is what they said to me:

Lady, turn around, turn around, turn around,

Lady, touch the ground, touch the ground, touch the ground,

Lady, tie your shoe, tie your shoe, tie your shoe,

Lady, that'll do, that'll do, that'll do.

Momma bear
Poppa bear
Daddy lost his underwear
Momma had another pair
One to wear
And one to spare.

"Fire, fire," said Mrs. McGuire,

"Where, where," said Mrs. O'Dare,

"Downtown," said Mrs. Brown,

"Heaven save us," said Mrs. O'Davis,

"Run, run," said Mrs. Dunn.

Jean, Jean had a machine
Joe, Joe made it go
Art, Art let a fart
And blew the engine all apart.

Mother, mother I am ill.
Send for the doctor
On the hill.
Send for the doctor,
Send for the nurse.
Send for the lady
With the alligator purse.

Fuzzy Wuzzy was a bear.
Fuzzy Wuzzy had no hair.
Fuzzy Wuzzy wasn't fuzzy.
Wuz he?

Once there was a little worm
Ooey was his name.
Ooey crossed the railroad tracks
And didn't see the train.

Now Ooey Gooey is the name
That suits him to the letter.
Too bad that he is not around.
He won't be getting better!

Quick, quick,
the cat's been sick!
Where? Where?
Under the chair.
Hasten, hasten,
Fetch the basin.
No, no, bring the po.
Kate, Kate,
It's way too late,
The carpet's in a dreadful state.

Auntie Mary, Auntie Mary,
Lost the leg of her drawers:
Uncle Willy, Uncle Willy,
Will you lend me yours?

A tutor who tooted the flute
Tried to tutor two tooters to toot.
Said the two to the tutor,
"Is it harder to toot, or
To tutor two tooters to toot?"

The sheet I slit
Was a well slit sheet!

Knock, knock,
Who's there?
Little old lady.
Little old lady who?
I didn't know you could yodel!

I started at the corner
I walked around the block
And I walked right into
A doughnut shop.
I pulled a doughnut
Out of the grease,
And gave the lady a five cent piece.
She looked at the nickel
And she looked at me.
She said, "This nickel's
No good to me.
There's a hole in the middle,
You can see right through."
Said I, "There's a hole
In your doughnut too!"
Shave and a haircut, two bits!

Make new friends
   but keep the old.
New friends are silver
   old friends are gold.

There are old ships,
There are new ships.
But the best ship
Is friendship.

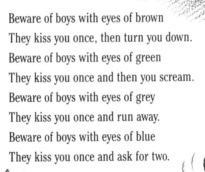

Beware of boys with eyes of brown
They kiss you once, then turn you down.
Beware of boys with eyes of green
They kiss you once and then you scream.
Beware of boys with eyes of grey
They kiss you once and run away.
Beware of boys with eyes of blue
They kiss you once and ask for two.

I scream, you scream,
We all scream for ice cream.

I love you, I love you,
I love you divine.
Give me your bubblegum,
You're chewing mine.

I hate you, I hate you,
I hate you clear through.
You stuck all the bubblegum,
Right to my shoe.

L'AMOUR

Kate and Brian
Sitting in a tree
K * I * S * S * I * N * G.
First comes love,
Then comes marriage,
Soon they'll come
With a baby carriage.

I love coffee
I love tea
I love the boys
And the boys love me.

You remind me of a man.
What man?
A hoodoo.
Who do?
You do.
What?
Remind me of a man.

I went upstairs
Just like me
I combed my hair
Just like me
I looked in the mirror
Just like me
I saw a monkey
Just like me

Don't look at me in that tone of voice!

Adam and Eve and Pinch-me
Went down to the river to bathe.
Adam and Eve got drowned.
Who do you think was saved?
Pinch Me!

Pinch-me, Punch-me and Tread-on-my-toes
Went down to the seaside to bathe.
Two of the three were drowned.
Choose who you think was saved!

I one the slimy worms.
  I two the slimy worms.
I three the slimy worms.
  I four the slimy worms.
I five the slimy worms.
  I six the slimy worms.
I seven the slimy worms.
  I...ATE the slimy worms!
Eee-ewww!

Friends I will remember you,
Think of you,
Sing for you.
And when the day is through,
I'll still be friends with you.

I see London
I see France
I see Jenny's
Dirty pants.

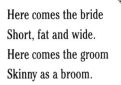

Here comes the bride
Short, fat and wide.
Here comes the groom
Skinny as a broom.

Here comes the bride
forty-five feet wide.
Slipped on a banana peel
And went for a ride.

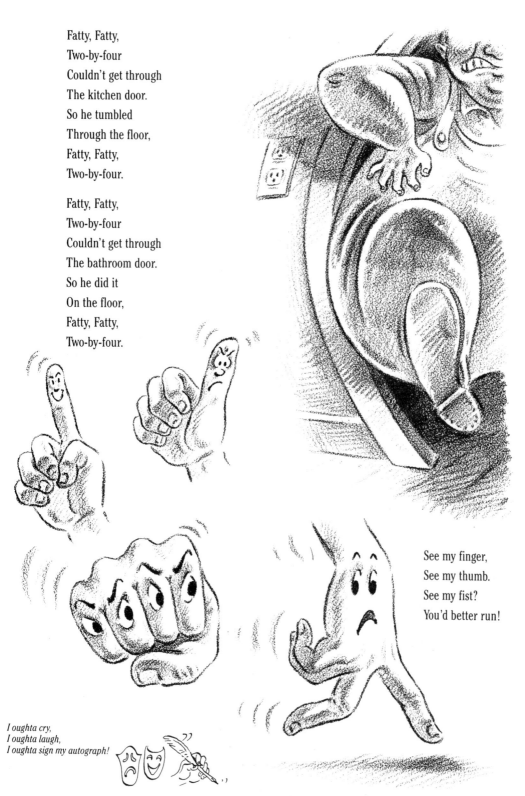

Fatty, Fatty,
Two-by-four
Couldn't get through
The kitchen door.
So he tumbled
Through the floor,
Fatty, Fatty,
Two-by-four.

Fatty, Fatty,
Two-by-four
Couldn't get through
The bathroom door.
So he did it
On the floor,
Fatty, Fatty,
Two-by-four.

See my finger,
See my thumb.
See my fist?
You'd better run!

I oughta cry,
I oughta laugh,
I oughta sign my autograph!

Liar, liar,
Pants on fire.
Pants got caught
On a telephone wire.

Sticks and stones
May break my bones,
But names will never hurt me.

Fingers were made before forks!

Made you look,
Made you stare,
Made the barber cut your hair
Cut it long, cut it short,
Cut it with a knife and fork.

Made you look,
You dirty crook
Stole your mother's pocket book.
Turned it in, turned it out,
Turned it into sauerkraut.

Made you look,
Made you stare,
Made you lose your underwear!

My teacher and a monkey
　　Were sitting on a rail.
The only difference I could see—
　　The monkey had a tail!

Our teacher and a donkey
　　Were calculating math.
The donkey won the contest—
　　Now tell me who's an ass!

If brains were dynamite, you'd be safe.

BE QUIET

SIT DOWN

OUT FOR SUMMER

No more pencils
No more books
No more teacher's
Dirty looks.

No more recess
No more friends
I think I might
Return again.

Happy birthday to you,
You live in a zoo,
You look like a monkey,
And you smell like one too.

Happy birthday to you,
Squashed tomatoes and stew,
Bread and butter in the gutter,
Happy birthday to you.

Fudge, fudge,
Tell the judge,
Mommy's had a baby.
Oh joy, it's a boy!
Daddy's going crazy.

Wrap it up in tissue paper,
Put it in the elevator.
Stop at one, stop at two,
My brother's gone,
What can you do?

Big stink,
What do you think?
Daddy's in a whirl.
I must explain that they're to blame,
They should have had a girl!

Tattle-tale, Tattle-tale
Tell-tale, Twit
Your nose will grow long
And your tongue shall be slit.

Tell-tale tit,
Your tongue shall be split,
And all the little puppy dogs
Shall have a little bit.

In your eye
With a pizza pie,
On your head
With an iron bed,
Up your nose
With a rubber hose,
Twice as far
With a chocolate bar!

Don't cut off your nose to spite your face.

Sing a little song,
Do a little dance,
When I drop this ice cube
Down your pants.

Don't you worry,
Don't you fret.
Chicken pox
Will get you yet!

Beg your pardon,
Grant your grace;
Hope the cat
Will spit in your face.

PARDON MOI!

Eenie-meanie-miney-mo
Catch a tiger by the toe.
If he hollers
Let him go
Eenie-meanie-miney-mo.

Boomelacka, Boomelacka,
Bow, wow, wow,
Chickelacka, Chickelacka,
Chow, chow, chow,
Ch-hee,
Ch-ho,
Ch-ha-ha,
We'll beat your team,
Rah, rah, rah!

He thinks he's the cat's whiskers.

25

One potato, two potato,
Three potato, four,
Five potato, six potato,
Seven potato more.

Bouncie bouncie ballie
I broke my sister's dolly
She gave me a whack
I paid her back
Bouncie bouncie ballie.

Pineapple custard,
Strawberry pie,
V * I * C * T * O * R * Y!

Lean to the left,
Lean to the right,
Stand up, sit down,
Fight! Fight! Fight!

One for the money
Two for the show
Three to get ready
Now go cat, go!

Here I sit a-sewing
In my little housie.
Nobody comes to see me
Except my little mousie.
So rise Sally, rise
And close up your eyes.
Point to the east
And point to the west.
And point to the very one
That you love best.

A tisket, a tasket,
A brown and yellow basket,
I wrote a letter to my love
And on the way I dropped it.
I dropped it, I dropped it,
And on the way I dropped it.
A little doggy picked it up
And put it in his pocket.
  I won't bite you,
  I won't bite you,
  I won't bite you,
  But I will bite you!

D-better.

D-sooner

D-letter

D-liver

One, two, three a-lary,
Lost my ball in City Dairy,
If you find it
Give it to Mary
One, two, three a-lary.

One, two, three a-lary,
My first name is Sherry.
If you think it's necessary
Look it up in the dictionary.
One, two, three a-lary.

Ordinary moving,
Laughing, talking,
One hand, the other hand,
One foot, the other foot,
Clap at the front,
Clap at the back,
Front and back,
Back and front,
Tweedles, twydles,
Salute to the king,
Bow to the queen,
And around we go.

*I'm the king of the castle
And you're the dirty rascal.*

Sam, Sam, Skateboard Sam,
Everybody knows just who I am.
  Can you do an Ollie?
Yes I can!
  Can you do a Taildrop?
Yes I can!
  Can you do a Boneless?
Man, oh man!
Everybody watch that Skateboard Sam.

Sam, Sam, Skateboard Sam,
Everybody knows just who I am.
  Can you do a Tear now?
Yes I can!
  Can you do a Spin Drop?
Yes I can!
  Can you do a Good Trick?
Man, oh man!
Everybody watch that Skateboard Sam.

Put your hands in your pockets,
Put your thumbs in your pants,
Watch the little turtle
Do the hootchie kootchie dance.

I was standing on the corner
   not doing any harm,
When along came a policeman
   and took me by the arm.

He took me to a little box
   and there he rang a bell.
Along came a cop car
   and took me to my cell.

When I woke up in the morning
   I looked up on the wall.
The spiders and the bedbugs
   were all playing ball.

The score was 19-20,
   the bedbugs were ahead.
The spiders hit a home run
   and knocked me out of bed.

The score was 20-20,
   no one was ahead.
And that was my adventure
   in my waterbed.

I called for the guard
   and said I wanted bail.
He got me a lawyer
   and now I'm out of jail!

My mother said
I never should
Play with the gypsies
In the wood.

If I did, she would say,
"Naughty girl, to disobey!
Disobey, disobey,
Naughty girl to disobey!"

Disobey one, disobey two,
Disobey cock-a-doodle-doo.

Girl Guide, Girl Guide
Dressed in blue,
These are the motions
You must do.
Stand at attention,
Stand at ease.
Bend your elbows,
Bend your knees.

Salute to the Captain,
Bow to the queen,
Turn your back on the dirty submarine.
I can do the heel-toe,
I can do the splits,
I can do the wiggle-waggle
Just like this.

Gabby had a steamboat,
The steamboat had a bell.
Gabby went to heaven,
The steamboat went to...
Hello operator,
Give me number nine.
If you don't connect me,
I'll kick your big...
Behind the 'frigerator
There was a piece of glass.
Gabby stepped upon it
And hurt her little...
Ask me no more questions,
I'll tell you no more lies.
The boys are in the washroom
Doing up their...
Flies are in the city,
Bees are in the park.
Gabby and her boyfriend
Are kissing in the...
D * A * R * K! Dark! Dark! Dark!
Dark is like a movie,
A movie's like a show.
A show is like a radio
And this is all I know!

I was going to the country
I was going to the fair,
I met a senorita
With flowers in her hair.
Shake it senorita,
Shake it all you can.
Shake it senorita,
Till you find a man.
Shake it to the bottom,
Shake it to the top,
Turn around, turn around,
Stop, stop, stop!

Knock, knock.
Who's there?
Elvis Presley's underwear.

Elvis Presley was a star
S * T * A * R.
He could do the go-go,
He could do the twist,
He could do the wiggle-jiggle,
Just like this!

Hurry Mr. Postman,
Don't be slow,
Be like Elvis Presley,
Go, man, go!

Knock, knock.

Who's there?

Eileen.

Eileen who?

Eileen Over.

A sailor went to sea sea sea
  to see what he could see see see
And all that he did see see see
  was the bottom of the sea sea sea.

Vote vote vote for dear old Lisa,
Who's that knocking at the door?
Lisa is the one
Who is having all the fun
So we won't vote for Lisa anymore.

Vote vote vote for dear old Norman,
Who's that knocking at the door?
If it's Norman let him in
And we'll sock him in the chin
And we won't vote for Norman anymore.

Two, four, shut the door, no more!

35

Teddy bear, teddy bear, turn around,
Teddy bear, teddy bear, touch the ground,
Teddy bear, teddy bear, tie your shoe,
Teddy bear, teddy bear, that will do,
Teddy bear, teddy bear, go upstairs,
Teddy bear, teddy bear, say your prayers,
Teddy bear, teddy bear, switch off the light,
Teddy bear, teddy bear, say goodnight.

All in together girls,
This fine weather girls,
Put your coats and jackets on,
Tell your moms you won't be long.
On your birthday month run out,
Now it's time to yell and shout:
January, February, March, April,
May, June, July, August,
September, October, November, December!

Cinderella
Dressed in yella
Went upstairs
To kiss a fella.
Made a mistake
And kissed a snake.
How many doctors
Did it take?
1, 2, 3, 4, 5, 6, 7, 8.

Blue bells, cockle shells
Eavie, ivy, over.
My mother sent me to the store
And this is what she sent me for:
Salt, sugar, coffee, beans, ham, eggs
and PEPPERS!

Dizzy Duck is a one-legged,
One-legged, one-legged duck.
Dizzy Duck is a two-legged,
Two-legged, two-legged duck.
Dizzy Duck is a three-legged,
Three-legged, three-legged duck.
Dizzy Duck is a four-legged,
Four-legged, four-legged Duck.
Dizzy Duck is a no-legged,
No-legged, no-legged duck.

I had a little sportscar
Two forty-eight
Went around the cor—ner
And slammed on the brake.
Policeman caught me
And put me in jail
All I had was gingerale.
PEPPERS! 10, 20, 30, 40, 50...

Come, come now playmate,
Come out and play with me
And bring your dollies three,
Climb up my apple tree,
Splash in my rain barrel,
Slide down my cellar door,
And we'll be jolly friends
Forevermore.

I'm sorry playmate,
I cannot play with you
My dollies have the flu,
Boo-hoo boo-hoo hoo-hoo,
Aint got no rain barrel,
Aint got no cellar door,
But we'll be jolly friends
Forevermore.

Stella ella ola
Clap, clap, clap,
Say est chingo chico
Chico chico chap
Say est chico chico
Hello, you're late,
Say 1,2,3,4,5,6,7,8!

There was an old man
Named Michael Finnigin
He grew whiskers on his chinigin
The wind came out
And blew them inigin
Poor old Michael Finnigin, beginigin.

There was an old man
Named Michael Finnigin
The preacher told him not to singigin
He went back to
Drinkin ginigin
Poor old Michael Finnigin, beginigin.

There was an old man
Named Michael Finnigin
Who bet on a horse and tried to winigin
The horse fell down
And broke its shinigin
Poor old Michael Finnigin, Finnigin.

Miss Mary Mac, Mac, Mac,
All dressed in black, black, black,
With silver buttons, buttons, buttons,
All down her back, back, back,
She asked her mother, mother, mother,
For fifty cents, cents, cents,
To watch the cows, cows, cows,
Jump over the fence, fence, fence,
They jumped so high, high, high,
They touched the sky, sky, sky,
They kept on going, going, going,
Till the first of July-ly-ly.

Miss Hetty Proctor
Sitting in a rocker
Eating soda crackers
Watching the clock go
Tick, tock,
Tick-tock sha walla-walla
Tick, tock,
Tick-tock sha walla-walla
A, B, C, D, E, F, G,
Wash those cooties offa me.
Moonshine! Moonshine!
Moonshine freeze!

Eenie meanie popsa-meanie
Oo-ah popsa-meanie
Education, liberation,
I love you.
Downtown baby,
Down by the roller coaster,
Sweet, sweet baby
Won't let ya go.
Caught ya with your boyfriend,
Naughty, naughty,
Didn't do the dishes,
Lazy, lazy,
Stole a piece of candy,
Greedy, greedy,
Jumped out the window,
Crazy, crazy,
Eenie meanie popsa-meanie
Oo-ah popsa meanie
Education, liberation,
I hate you.

Hump dee-dump,
Hump-hump dee dumpty dumpty,
Hump dee-dump,
Hump-hump dee dumpty dumpty

Mary had a little lamb
Its fleece was white as snow,
And everywhere that Mary went,
Hunh! Aint that funky now.

Hump dee-dump,
Hump-hump dee dumpty-dumpty,
Hump dee-dump,
Hump-hump dee dumpty-dumpty

Jack and Jill went up the hill
To fetch a pail of water,
Jack fell down and broke his crown,
Hunh! Aint that funky now.

Hump dee-dump,
Hump-hump dee dumpty dumpty,
Hump dee-dump,
Hump-hump dee dumpty dumpty

Simple Simon met a pieman
Going to the fair,
Said Simple Simon to the pieman
Hunh! Aint that funky now.

Yours till Niagara falls

She sells sea shells by the seashore.
And the sea shells that she sells
Are seashore shells I'm sure.

Step on a crack
And break your mother's back.
Step in a space
And kiss her on the face.

Step on a nail
And send her to jail.
Step on a bee
You'll break her knee.

But step in a puddle
And you're in trouble!

Our country is a free land
Free without a doubt
If you have no cash for lunch
You're free to go without.

Yours till I drink Canada dry

44

Spring has sprung,
The grass has riz,
I wonder where
The birdies is?
They say the bird
Is on the wing,
But that's absurd,
I say the wing
Is on the bird.

Birdie, birdie in the sky,
Dropping whitewash in my eye.
But I don't weep,
And I don't cry,
I'm just glad that cows don't fly.

See a pin and pick it up
    All the day
You'll have good luck.

See a pin and let it lie
    You'll be sorry
By and by.

All the fine compliments
And all the fine wishes
Never replace
Help with the dishes.

Knock, knock.
Who's there?
Ach.
Ach who?
Bless you!

Lucky lucky white horse,
Lucky lucky Lee,
Lucky lucky white horse,
Lucky lucky me!

I think that there could never be
A thing more lovely than a tree
But if the tree should fall on me
I'd like to change my mind!

In fourteen hundred and ninety-two
Columbus sailed the ocean blue.
He sailed so far
On the deep blue sea
That he didn't come back
Till fourteen ninety-three!

Dinosaur, dinosaur,
Where did you go?
Where did you come from?
Who did you know?

Je t'adore, dinosaur

White socks, they always get dirty,
The longer you wear them
The dirtier they get.
Sometimes I think of the laundry,
But something keeps telling me
Oh, no, not yet.

Black socks, they never get dirty,
The longer you wear them
The cleaner they get.
Sometimes I think I should wash them,
But something keeps telling me
Oh, no, not yet.

Good, better, best,
Never let it rest,
Till your good is better
And your better, best.

Mississauga rattlesnake
   Eat brown bread.
Mississauga rattlesnake
   Fall down dead.
If you catch a caterpillar
   Feed it apple juice.
If you catch a rattlesnake
   Turn him loose!
Gimme a break, gimme a break,
   Gimme a break, rattlesnake!

On top of spaghetti
All covered in cheese
I lost my poor meatball
When somebody sneezed.
It rolled off the table
And onto the floor
And then my poor meatball
Rolled out of the door.
It rolled in the garden
And under a bush
And then my poor meatball
Was nothing but mush.
So if you like spaghetti
All covered in cheese
Hold onto your meatballs
And don't ever sneeze.

Beans, beans the musical fruit,
The more you eat, the more you toot.
The more you toot, the more you fart,
Beans, beans, they're good for the heart.

Beans, beans, good for the heart,
The more you eat, the more you fart.
The more you toot, the better you feel,
So let's have beans at every meal.

Jelly in the bowl,
Jelly in the bowl,
Wiggle woggle,
Wiggle woggle,
Jelly in the bowl.

Pizza on my plate,
Pizza on my plate,
Gibble gobble,
Gibble gobble,
Just couldn't wait.

Nobody likes me, everybody hates me,
I'm gonna go eat worms.
Big fat juicy ones,
Eeny-weeny-squeemy ones,
See how they wiggle and squirm.
Chop off their heads,
And squeeze out the juice,
And throw the tails away.
Nobody knows how I survive
On worms three times a day!

The cookie crumbles here,
The cookie crumbles there.
It crumbles in your pocket,
It crumbles in your hair.

Never say die till a dead horse kicks you.

It crumbles in the car,
It crumbles on the floor.
Don't sweep the cookie crumbs
Underneath the door.

Don't sweep the cookie crumbs
Underneath the rug.
They might become a snack
For a BIG FAT BUG.

CRUNCH!!

I eat my peas with honey,
I've done it all my life.
It makes the peas taste funny,
But it keeps them on my knife.

Burgers and chips,
Burgers and chips,
Whenever I eat them
They go to my hips.

Pizza and fries,
Pizza and fries,
They call to my tummy
And light up my eyes.

Candy and gum,
Candy and gum,
Whenever I have it
It sticks to my bum.

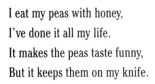

My mom gave me a penny
To go and see Jack Benny
I did not see Jack Benny
I bought some chewing gum.

My mom gave me a nickel
To go and buy a pickle
I did not buy a pickle
I bought some chewing gum.

My mom gave me a dime
To go and buy a lime
I did not buy a lime
I bought some chewing gum.

My mom gave me a quarter
To go and pay the porter
I did not pay the porter
I bought some chewing gum.

My mom gave me a dollar
To go and buy a collar
I did not buy a collar
I bought some chewing gum.

My mom gave me two dollars
To go and buy some chewing gum
I did not buy some chewing gum
I'm sick of chewing gum!

Na na-na na-na chewing gum
Na na-na na-na chewing gum
Na na-na na-na chewing gum
I'm sick of chewing gum!

Supersaurus
Ultrasaurus
Spinosaurus too.

Allosaurus
Stegosaurus
All were eating stew.

Oviraptor
Baryonix
Came upon the scene.

They shook their tails
They showed their teeth
And licked the platter clean.

Got a cold?
Don't worry.
Chicken soup
In a hurry!

Got it made, lemonade,
Hello, hello, bowl of jello,
No dice, orange slice,
Got a hunch, carrot bunch,
Holy Hannah, top banana,
What a dud, boiled spud,
So what, kumquat,
Lost your mind, melon rind,
Upon my soul, cabbage roll,
Make a scene, tangerine,
Way to go, ripe mango,
What's your rush, oatmeal mush,
Whaddya mean, jellybean,
Don't you mutter, peanut butter,
All right, vegemite,
What a nerd, bean curd,
Unreal, banana peel,
Gimme a break, T-bone steak,
Peachy keen, coffee bean,
Slurp, crunch, munch,
That was lunch.

What are the three rudest vegetables?
Lettuce, turnip and pea.

Milk is binding,
So is cheese,
Eat fresh fruit
And work with ease.

Pardon me for being so rude,
It was not me, it was my food.

Alice, if you're able,
Get your elbows off the table,
This is not a horse's stable
But a first-class dining table.
Stand up! Say you're sorry!

Past my teeth and over my tongue,
Look out stomach, here it comes!

Good night
Sleep tight
Don't let
The bedbugs bite.

Good night
Darkness grows
Lie on your back
Don't squash your nose.

Good night
Sweet repose
Hope the fleas
Don't bite your nose.

Good night
Pleasant dreams
Don't let nightmares
Make you scream.

You're a sight for sore eyes.

55

Star light
Star bright
First star I see tonight
I wish I may
I wish I might
Have the wish
I wish tonight.

Now I lay me down to sleep
A bag of candy at my feet.
If I should die before I wake
You'll know I died of stomach ache.

I see sights
In the middle of the night!

There's no need to light a night-light
On a light night like tonight.
For a night-light's a slight light
On a light night like tonight.

Adios amoebas!